Snowfall at Cedar Hollow

A Cedar Hollow Love Story

By

Susan Trott

Susan Trott

Copyright

Published by **TaggerPress**
Ottawa, Canada
taggerpress.ca

ISBN: 978-1-998107-50-6

Printed in the United States of America / Canada
First Edition, Ingram

Cover Design: Susan Trott & Virelith
Interior Layout: Susan Trott
Artwork: Generated with assistance from AI design tools

For more books by the author, visit:
taggerpress.com

Dedication

To all the lovers out there dreaming of their perfect someone.

May your hearts find their way.

Table of Contents

Chapter 1

Recalculating

The snow started halfway through the last hour of the drive. Harper Lane watched it drift toward her on the windshield, lazy at first, then steadier, knitting itself into a white curtain that turned the highway into a tunnel. Her wipers thumped a tired rhythm, smearing road salt into pastel streaks. The GPS on the dash glowed in the growing dark, its digital voice cheerfully oblivious to the gnawing in her chest.

"Continue for forty-five kilometers," it suggested.

"Continue where?" Harper muttered. "Into the void?"

Her coffee was lukewarm and sour. Her shoulders ached from hunching over a keyboard for the last... what, fifteen years? Twenty? New York felt like it was pressed into the muscles of her neck. Book tours, signings, panels, interviews. Photos of her smiling so hard her jaw hurt, while somewhere, deep inside, the part of her that used to love stories quietly curled up and slept.

She glanced at the passenger seat.

Her laptop bag sat there like a reproachful pet. Inside, waiting in the dim electric warmth of hard drive and RAM, was a Word file named *Winter's Reckoning – First Draft*.

It contained exactly nine pages.

Eight of those were false starts. One was a grocery list.

Her phone chimed with a text from Mara. Harper didn't need to look to know what it would say. She could hear her editor's voice in her head:

> **You've got this. This is just a little block. You need oxygen, that's all. Go. Breathe. Write. Call me when you have five chapters. ❤**

Mara meant well. Mara always meant well. And Mara had been the one to book this "emergency retreat" when Harper confessed over a rare, unguarded glass of wine that she hadn't written more than a few usable pages in months.

"You need out," Mara had said. "Out of the apartment, out of the overstimulation, out of the city. I'm sending you to a cottage. It's quiet, it's snowy, it has Wi-Fi and a fireplace and an aggressively charming town nearby. You'll hate it for three days and then you'll write like you used to."

The GPS chimed again. "Turn right in eight hundred meters."

A hand-painted sign loomed out of the snow ahead:

CEDAR HOLLOW – 2 MILES

YOU'RE ALMOST HOME

Home. That was generous.

Harper flicked on her turn signal anyway.

The exit lane curved away from the main highway and into a narrower road flanked by dark spruce and birch. Snow caught in the tree branches, softening every edge. Her breath fogged in the car, and she turned the heat up a notch, listening to the fan whine and the snow hiss under her tires.

She realized, abruptly, that she couldn't hear any traffic behind her.

For the first time in longer than she could remember, she was the only car on the road.

The thought was both terrifying and oddly… lightening. As if the city's constant chorus of engines and sirens had been a soundtrack she hadn't known she was desperate to switch off.

The trees thinned, and Cedar Hollow appeared like someone had shaken the snow globe and set it gently on a mantel.

A main street lined with brick and clapboard storefronts. Wreaths on the lampposts, big old-fashioned ones with red velvet bows. A bakery with fogged-up windows and a painted sign that declared:

HOLLOW BREADS & SWEETS.

A hardware store, a florist, something with guitars in the window.

Strings of lights crisscrossed above the road, blurred halos in the snowfall. A banner sagged cheerfully under the weight of white, its letters just visible as she crept past:

CEDAR HOLLOW WINTERFEST & BOOK FAIR – DECEMBER 23

Harper's stomach did an odd little lurch at the word *book.* She drove on.

The GPS guided her around a bend and up a side street of small houses, each one wearing its own variation of holiday cheer—icicle lights, glowing reindeer, a plastic snowman army standing guard on a lawn. At the end of the lane, past a row of tall pines, stood her destination: a two-story house with pale siding, a deep front porch, and a driveway that looked like it had been shoveled by someone who did not consider "evenness" a priority.

She parked with care and sat for a moment, hands still on the wheel.

Snow ticked softly on the roof. In the side mirror, the town's lights were a warm blur. The dashboard clock read 4:38 p.m., but the sky had already slid into that blue-gray twilight that made everything look like the inside of a memory.

"Okay," she told herself. "You can do this. It's just... a house. A house with no noisy neighbors. No sirens. No delivery people ringing the buzzer six times for the wrong apartment.

Just you and your laptop and some pretentious herbal tea you bought for this exact performance."

She grabbed her coat, her laptop bag, and the overnight duffel that represented Mara's stern instructions to "pack cozy, not presentable." Her boots crunched into the shallow drift as she stepped out. The air hit her face—cold, clean, carrying the faint smell of woodsmoke from somewhere nearby.

Harper inhaled, deeper than she meant to.

The cold burned sweetly in her lungs. For a second, something inside her loosened.

She trudged up the path, key from the rental company clutched in her gloved hand, and wrestled the front door open. The house greeted her with darkness, the faint tick of old heating, and the smell of pine cleaner overlaying something older and homier—baked bread, maybe. Or time.

The interior was simple but charming: hardwood floors, a mishmash of furniture that somehow worked, a stone fireplace with a mantel begging for stockings. The kind of place that would have photographed well for a magazine spread titled *City Weary? Try Rustic Minimalism.*

She dumped her bags in the front hall, kicked off her boots, and padded through to the back of the house, drawn by a soft glow leaking around the edge of a pair of sliding glass doors.

She reached for the curtain and tugged it aside.

Her first clear look at the backyard knocked the breath out of her.

A wooden pergola framed the night sky, its beams dusted with snow. Round bulbs were strung in graceful lines overhead, casting pools of warm, honey-coloured light onto the patio below. Outdoor chairs and a long table stood under thick white drifts, their once-sharp edges rounded into gentle, snowy shapes. Beyond the pergola, a cluster of trees shimmered with blue fairy lights, turning the falling snowflakes into tiny comets.

The world beyond the glass door was quiet. Not the false quiet of noise-cancelling headphones, but a deep, padded stillness that seemed to soak into the bones of the place.

Harper leaned one hand against the doorframe.

"Okay, Mara," she whispered. "You win. This is… ridiculous."

She opened the door a crack. Cold air slipped in, along with the soft, almost inaudible sound of snow landing on snow. The lights outside hummed faintly. Somewhere to her right, a faint creaking sound suggested the presence of a fence, or maybe a tree swaying under its new white burden.

The house behind her was a shadowy reflection on the glass. Her face hovered there too, framed by the glow of her phone screen in one hand, hair coming loose from the messy knot she'd shoved it into that morning.

For the first time in months, she didn't look… harried. Just tired. But there was something else there, too. An echo of the woman who had once stayed up all night because the story in her head was too bright and insistent to ignore.

Maybe it was the lights. Or the snow. Or the fact that for the first time since her first book, nobody in this town had any expectations of her yet.

She opened the door wider and stepped out onto the patio.

The cold wrapped around her ankles immediately, sneaking under the cuffs of her jeans. Snow squeaked under her socks. She laughed out loud, half at herself, half at the absurdity of stepping outside without shoes like some kind of deranged elf.

She turned in a slow circle under the pergola, head tipped back, watching the flakes drift down through the glowing bulbs. If she squinted, the world narrowed to light, snow, breath.

She could almost feel a story stirring somewhere in the back of her mind, not yet words, just—

Something rustled under the deck.

Harper froze.

The deck ran along the back of the house, a few feet off the ground, supported by wooden posts. The space underneath was dark, the kind of dark that swallowed the light instead of merely resisting it.

The rustling came again. Louder. Something bumped against a beam.

Harper's brain supplied a rapid slideshow of possibilities: raccoon, skunk, bear, serial killer, the physical manifestation of her procrastination.

"Hello?" she called, because evidently she had learned nothing from horror movies.

The rustling paused.

She took a cautious step closer to the edge of the deck, peering into the gloom. Snow had drifted partway under the overhang, but beyond that, it was just shadow and the suggestion of movement.

"Uh... if you're a raccoon, please be friendly," she added. "If you're a murderer, this is a terrible place to pick, I have, like, no marketable organs."

A muffled male voice drifted up from the dark.

"Easy there, I'm just trying to rescue a cat."

Harper stared.

For a heartbeat, she thought she'd imagined it. Then a shape shifted under the deck; a boot scraping wood, the glint of metal, a hand sliding forward to push aside a low-hanging lattice.

"Did you say... a cat?" she managed.

There was a soft clink as the unseen stranger nudged something further into the shadows. A bowl? A tin?

"Yeah," the voice said. Closer now. Warm, faintly amused. "White. Cranky. Been hiding under here since the snow started. I've almost got—"

His head emerged into the spill of light, followed by a pair of broad shoulders in a dark jacket, dusted with snow. He squinted up at her, eyes adjusting, and for a moment they just stared at each other: Harper in her socks and city coat, breath puffing out in little clouds; the stranger half-kneeling under her deck, holding a battered tin of tuna and looking unreasonably handsome for someone caught in the act of trespassing.

Harper tightened her grip on the doorframe.

"Of course," she said faintly. "I leave New York to get away from the weird, and my rental comes with a basement cat smuggler."

A small white shape slipped out from under the deck behind him, tail flicking, ears pinned back in icy disdain. The cat slunk past his knee, gave Harper a long, considering look, and then hopped daintily onto one of the snow-capped chairs beneath the pergola as if to say, *At last. You're late.*

The man followed the cat's gaze back to Harper and smiled, slow and apologetic.

"Sorry," he said, shifting his weight and rising carefully to his feet. "Didn't mean to startle you. I'm Jack. Your, uh—" He gestured vaguely toward the hedge dividing the properties. "Next-door neighbor. And part-time feline negotiator."

Snowflakes settled on his hair. The cat blinked regally at them both.

Harper looked from Jack to the cat to the glowing pergola lights and back again, feeling the surrealness of the moment prickling her skin.

She had wanted quiet.

Instead, on her first night in Cedar Hollow, she had acquired a neighbor, a stray cat, and the beginning of something that felt suspiciously like a scene in one of her own books.

For the first time in a very long time, Harper Lane didn't mind at all.

Chapter 2
The Hollow Bookshop

Harper woke to the unmistakable sound of silence. Not the muted hum of city life, not the arguing radiators, not the neighbor's dog conducting heated debates with delivery drivers.

Just... silence.

Thick, soft, enveloping. The kind you could lean your whole body into.

For a moment she lay still, blinking up at the faint winter light pressed against the curtains. The house around her creaked and sighed; the deep, settling sounds of old timber and colder weather. It felt like a place that breathed.

And then the memories of the night before slid neatly back into place.

Snow.

The pergola lights.

A white cat with an alarming sense of ownership.

A man emerging from beneath her deck like a forest guardian with good hair.

Jack.

Harper groaned and shoved her face into the flannel pillow.

"Oh God. I threatened a stranger with a broom."

The house did not judge. But it didn't offer sympathy either.

Eventually she sat up, wrapped herself in a borrowed quilt, and padded to the back door. Snow drifted lazily outside, clinging to the glass. That's when she saw them:

Little pawprints circling the patio like a spiral.

Looping.

Pausing.

Contemplating the mysteries of existence under a deck chair.

"Snowball," Harper whispered experimentally.

It fit. Regal. Narcissistic. Fully aware she now owned the lease.

A long, dramatic growl from Harper's stomach reminded her she was human and required sustenance. After a shower and the triumphant discovery of a coffeemaker, she pulled on boots, a thick scarf, and the knitted hat she'd bought from a Brooklyn vendor who'd sworn it would "change her energy."

Maybe it would finally earn its keep.

A text from Mara lit her phone:

"Day 1: Don't panic. Or do, but write it down."

Harper snorted a laugh.

Outside, the snowfall had eased to a soft, drifting curtain. Fresh powder squeaked beneath her feet. The Rhys house looked even more like a postcard in daylight; snow-tipped roofline, frost edging the windows, the pergola lights still faintly glowing under the weight of winter.

Jack wasn't outside.

Not that she was looking.

She absolutely was.

On her walk toward town, a few neighbors waved. She waved back, startled at how easily her arm lifted. How normal it felt.

Main Street appeared like a watercolor in the morning light. It had soft edges, warm windows, woodsmoke curling from chimneys. Someone scraped ice from a shop sign. A kid attempted to sled down what barely counted as a hill. Bells jingled as the café door opened, releasing a drift of cinnamon-scented air.

And then she saw it.

The Hollow Bookshop.

Painted deep green with gold lettering curling like winter vines along the awning. The display window glowed warmly, arranged in miniature snowy scenes: paper trees, cotton batting, tiny sleigh figurines. In the center, a hand-lettered sign:

NEW ARRIVALS – COZY STORIES FOR COZY DAYS

and beneath it, as if the universe had a sense of humor—

Harper Lane – In Stock Now!

Harper groaned softly. "Perfect. Just perfect."

She pushed open the door. A bell chimed delicately.

Warmth washed over her; pine candles, old books, fresh scones. Paper stars hung overhead, swaying gently in the warm air.

Behind the counter stood a woman in her seventies with silver hair pinned loosely, reading glasses perched low on her nose, and the expression of someone who had survived much and chosen delight anyway.

When she looked up, her eyes widened.

"Well now," she breathed. "If it isn't Harper Lane."

Harper blinked. "I uh, sorry, how do you—"

The woman stepped out from behind the counter with impressive speed for someone wearing crocheted slippers.

"I'm Eloise Hart," she declared. "This is my kingdom." She gestured to the shelves with all the grandeur of presenting a castle. "And you, my dear, are on at least a dozen of them."

Heat rose to Harper's cheeks. "Right. I didn't expect anyone here to—"

"To know you?" Eloise finished. "Darling, Cedar Hollow is not cut off from culture. We have Wi-Fi and opinions."

Harper laughed despite herself.

"Are you here visiting?" Eloise continued. "Passing through? On a secret bookish quest? Please tell me you're writing something new."

"Well—"

"Oh goodness, forgive me." Eloise patted her arm. "Authors don't wander in every day. Living ones, I mean. We keep the others on the Local History shelf out of respect."

Harper blinked. "I... I'm staying on the edge of town for a bit. Trying to work."

Eloise's eyes sparked. "The Rhys house?"

Harper nodded.

"Oh lovely place," Eloise mused. "Drafty, magical, possibly haunted by a friendly ghost with knitting skills. You'll be fine."

Then she leaned in, voice dropping.

"And the neighbor's not bad either."

Harper nearly swallowed her tongue. "Wh—what?"

"Jack Reynolds," Eloise said with a knowing sigh. "The man looks like he was hand-carved by a lumberjack romance cover artist."

Harper tried not to choke. "We met briefly. He… rescued a cat."

"Of course he did," Eloise said fondly. "That stray has manipulated half this town into servitude. Has it adopted you yet?"

"I'm not sure 'adopted' is the right—"

"Oh, it is," Eloise said gravely. "You'll know."

Before Harper could reply, the bell chimed again.

Jack stepped inside, brushing snow from his coat.

He froze when he saw her.

She froze when she saw him.

Eloise's eyes lit like she'd just been handed front-row tickets to the world's slowest enemies-to-lovers arc.

"You're here early," Harper managed.

"You're here," Jack said softly, as if the observation carried weight.

Eloise clapped once, delighted.

"Jack! Perfect timing. Help me convince Harper to join the WinterFest book fair."

Jack raised an eyebrow. "You ambushed her already?"

"I invited with enthusiasm."

Harper sighed. "I don't know if I'm—"

"She should," Jack said, surprising both of them.

"It's a good event. And the town would love it."

Harper stared at him. "Since when are you the WinterFest authority?"

He shrugged. "I build half of it."

Eloise gasped. "Oh! Speaking of which, Jack's inspired this year's outdoor reading pergola."

Harper blinked. "My pergola?"

Jack pocketed his gloves. "It's a good space. Figured it might bring a little magic."

Harper's stomach did an unsettling swoop.

Eloise produced a flyer with a flourish.

"WinterFest is two weeks away! Readings, signings, children's events... and hopefully Harper Lane."

"No pressure," Jack added softly, eyes warm.

Harper exhaled. "I... might think about it."

Eloise beamed like she had secured Taylor Swift.

"Wonderful! Cocoa?"

"Yes," Harper said. "Please."

As Eloise bustled away, Harper turned to Jack.

"She's... a lot."

"She's harmless," he murmured. "Mostly."

Snow drifted past the windows. Books glowed under warm lamps. And Harper felt something shift inside her, something small but sure.

A click.

A loosening.

A beginning.

She had come here to hide.

But maybe, just maybe, Cedar Hollow was a place where she could be found.

Chapter 3

A Neighbor Made of Quiet Sparks

By the time Harper stepped back outside, the sky had shifted from pale morning to bright winter blue. Sunlight glinted off crusted snow, casting everything in a faint, glittering haze.

She cradled a paper bag from the bookshop against her chest — Eloise had insisted she leave with at least three "mood-regulating" books, and Harper hadn't had the heart (or spine) to argue.

The town bustled gently around her. A pair of teenagers were stringing more lights across a shop window. A man in a parka was brushing snow off a bench with exaggerated fury. A dog with a jaunty red sweater bounded past, dragging its owner toward the bakery with a sense of entitlement Harper deeply respected.

As she approached her rental house, she spotted a familiar figure near the hedge separating the property from the neighboring yard.

Jack Reynolds.

Again.

He was clearing snow from the walkway that cut alongside the houses , broad shoulders moving steadily, shovel scraping with decisive, practiced efficiency. His breath fogged in the air. A knit cap covered his dark hair, but a few strands had escaped, frosting lightly with snow.

He looked up as Harper approached and paused, leaning on the shovel handle.

"Well," he said with a crooked smile. "You survived the night in the wilderness."

Harper snorted. "Barely. I had to fend off a blanket that kept trying to smother me. Fierce creature."

His smile widened, slow and warm. "I've had similar encounters."

Harper stopped a few feet away, the cold air nibbling at her cheeks. Jack's presence was... easy. Calming. Grounded in a way she rarely encountered in New York, where everyone vibrated on twelve different frequencies of anxiety.

"Thanks again for rescuing the cat," she said.

"Snowball," Jack said immediately.

"I'm sorry?"

"That's her name." Jack stabbed the shovel gently into the snow. "Or at least the name she tolerates."

"Tolerates," Harper repeated, amused. "She seemed… opinionated."

Jack huffed a quiet laugh. "She is. Likes tuna, hates everyone until the eighth meeting. You got lucky. She usually doesn't reveal herself for at least a week."

Harper blinked. "She was pretty fast to judge me last night."

"That's not judgment," Jack corrected. "Trust me, you'll know judgment when she gives it." He lowered his voice conspiratorially. "She once peed in the mayor's boots."

Harper burst out laughing. The sound startled her. It had been a while since something made her laugh like that, sharp, sudden, real.

Jack watched her with an expression she couldn't quite read. Not amusement exactly, but something softer. Like he was cataloging the sound, or tucking it away.

"You heading out somewhere?" he asked, nodding at the paper bag in her arms.

"Oh, right. I visited the bookshop. Eloise armed me with reading material in case the writing goes… poorly."

"Does it go poorly often?"

Harper hesitated, a familiar pinch tightening her ribs. "Lately? It goes nowhere."

Jack studied her for a beat, then nodded. Not pitying, not prying, just acknowledging. It was strangely comforting.

"Well," he said finally, "if you need a place with fewer distractions than the house, my workshop's always warm. And the Wi-Fi actually works."

"Does mine not?"

Jack gave her a sympathetic grimace. "Rhys never fixed the router. It flickers like a haunted candle when the temperature drops."

Harper groaned. "Of course it does."

He chuckled. "Offer stands."

A puff of cold air drifted between them. Harper shifted her weight, suddenly aware of the sharpness of the winter day and the softness of Jack's expression.

"Well," she said lightly, "if I end up on your doorstep begging for functioning internet, try not to look too smug about it."

"No promises," he said.

She was turning to go when something white flickered in her peripheral vision.

Snowball, perched atop the fence like a tiny Arctic queen, blinked down at Jack and then, unmistakably, at Harper.

With slow, regal precision, she hopped down, trotted toward Harper with the confidence of someone who knew she owned the land, and sat neatly on Harper's boot.

Harper stared. "Uh…"

Jack's eyebrows lifted. "Oh. Wow. That's… early."

"What's early?"

Snowball pressed her forehead lightly against Harper's shin.

"That," Jack said. "That's a claim."

"A claim?" Harper repeated.

Jack nodded solemnly. "Snowball has chosen you."

Snowball meowed, a single, imperious sound that translated roughly to *You may serve me now.*

"Oh no," Harper whispered. "I have been annexed."

Jack burst into laughter, shaking his head. "I hope you weren't planning to sleep in. She likes breakfast at six."

Snowball trotted past Harper toward the house, tail held high like a fluffy exclamation point.

Harper sighed. "Do I need to sign something? A treaty?"

Jack leaned on the shovel. "Nope. Your fate is sealed. Congratulations, you're hers now."

Harper watched Snowball sit primly at the back door, waiting to be let in.

"This wasn't on the rental listing," Harper muttered.

Jack smiled. "Cedar Hollow rarely tells you everything. But it tends to give you what you need."

Something warm tugged at Harper's chest. She wasn't ready to examine it, so she nodded at Jack instead.

"I'll, uh… see you around?"

"Count on it," he said softly.

As Harper approached the house, Snowball darted inside with the confidence of someone entering her own kingdom. Harper followed, closing the door behind them as the warmth of the house wrapped around her again.

She set her books on the table, rubbed her hands together, and watched Snowball leap onto an armchair like a veteran claiming her throne.

It wasn't what Harper expected.

It wasn't anything she'd planned.

But for the first time in a long time, she didn't feel like she was running from something.

She felt like she was… arriving.

Chapter 4
Words, Wishes, and Untamed Wi-Fi

Snowball had opinions about Harper's morning routine. Harper discovered this by accident, when she dared—*dared*—to take a cup of coffee to the dining table before opening a can of cat food. Snowball sat on the chair opposite her, tail swishing like a metronome of judgment.

"I have been here for twelve hours," Harper said, pointing her spoon at the cat. "Twelve. And you already run the place."

Snowball blinked.

Harper sighed, set down her coffee, and went to the kitchen to retrieve a can. The moment the metal tab flicked up, Snowball trotted to her bowl with the brisk confidence of a CEO arriving for her morning briefing.

Once the cat was fed, Harper settled at the table with her laptop, hoping—desperately—that the glow of a fresh document would ignite some spark inside her.

The cursor blinked.

And blinked.

And blinked.

"Come on," she whispered. "Just a sentence. One sentence."

She typed:

The snow fell silently, like a thousand erased regrets.

She stared at it.

It was... okay. A little dramatic. A little purple. A little *Harper Lane trying too hard to remind herself she still has a voice.*

She deleted it.

"Ugh."

Snowball meowed sympathetically, though Harper suspected it was a request for seconds.

She tried again.

Winter crept over the city like—

The Wi-Fi icon on her laptop flickered.

Then vanished.

Harper groaned, forehead landing on the table with a soft thud.

Of course.

She opened her phone. No signal. None. Just the mocking little symbol of a lonely, disconnected world.

"Rhys," she muttered to the previous owner. "You had sixty-five years to fix the router and you chose violence."

Snowball hopped onto the table and sat on the keyboard.

"That doesn't help," Harper said.

Snowball blinked twice and then, very deliberately, pressed the space bar.

The screen illuminated with:

(a blinking cursor)

Harper exhaled. "Fine. I'm going to the workshop."

Snowball followed her to the door.

"You're not coming," Harper said sternly.

Snowball stared.

"You have food."

Snowball stared harder.

"I don't know if Jack likes cats in his workshop."

Snowball reviewed this. Then, like a ghost, vanished behind the couch—her version of a compromise.

Harper grabbed her coat and gloves, pulled her hat over her ears, and stepped outside into a bright, crystalline morning. The snow squeaked under her boots, sparkling in the low winter sun.

Jack's workshop sat behind his house, a stand-alone building with large windows and a slanted metal roof. Smoke curled from a small chimney at one end, and the warm glow of lights gleamed through frosted glass.

She hesitated halfway up the path, suddenly aware of how... intimate it felt to approach a man's workspace completely uninvited.

He offered, she reminded herself. *And you need Wi-Fi like oxygen.*

She raised her hand and knocked on the wooden door.

Inside, something whirred to a stop. Footsteps. Then the door opened, revealing Jack in sleeves rolled up to his elbows, hair mussed, face lightly dusted with sawdust.

He looked... delicious. And surprised.

But pleasantly so.

"Morning," he said, leaning casually against the doorframe. "Let me guess, the router died heroically in the line of duty."

"Tragically," Harper agreed. "There were no survivors."

Jack laughed, stepping aside. "Come on in."

The workshop felt like stepping into a warm, aromatic heartbeat. The heat from a small woodstove radiated through the space. Cedar shavings curled across the floor like golden ribbons. Tools hung neatly on the walls, and half-finished pieces of furniture occupied the center, tables, chairs, a headboard with carved stars.

Harper inhaled deeply. "Wow. This smells like... competence."

Jack arched a brow. "Competence?"

"And trees. Very... trustworthy trees."

He chuckled. "I'll take it."

He motioned toward a large wooden worktable near the window. A stool sat beside it, draped with a flannel cushion, and a small electric kettle perched on a corner shelf alongside mugs and a tin of tea.

"You can set up here," he said. "Wi-Fi password is 'cedarhands,' all lowercase."

"That's very lumberjack of you."

Jack grinned. "I strive to meet expectations."

Harper set her laptop down, relieved to see the familiar network pop up. The connection snapped in instantly, strong, steady, blessed. Heaven.

Jack returned to the piece he was sanding, a small side table with copper detailing. He worked with relaxed precision, movements smooth and practiced. The workshop felt like an extension of him: quiet, steady, capable.

Harper opened her document again.

Chapter One – Winter's Reckoning

The cursor blinked on an empty page.

No pressure.

No deadlines.

Just… stillness.

She breathed, fingers hovering.

Then she typed:

Snow fell across the city like a soft confession, covering everything it touched in a silence too gentle to refuse.

Jack glanced over from his workbench. "That sounds good."

Harper blinked. "You heard that?"

"I hear everything in this room," he said with a wink. "It's the acoustics."

Her cheeks warmed. "It's just a start."

"It's a good start," he said.

There was no flattery in it. No agenda.

Just truth.

Something small and tentative unfurled in her chest.

The workshop hummed with activity, the soft scrape of sandpaper, the crackle of the stove, the tap-tap of Harper's keys as she typed another line, then another.

For the first time in months, the words didn't feel extracted. They flowed. Clumsy at first, then smoother, like a frostbitten river remembering how to run.

She became dimly aware of Jack watching her again.

"What?" she asked, self-conscious.

He shrugged. "You look… lighter."

She swallowed. "I feel… something."

He set down his sandpaper, leaning against the bench. "Maybe this place is good for you."

"Or maybe your router is," Harper said, smiling.

The door creaked open suddenly, letting in a gust of cold air, and a small white cat who trotted inside like she owned the deed to the property.

"Snowball!" Jack yelped. "You don't even like me in here."

Snowball ignored him, leapt onto Harper's lap, and curled up with absolute authority.

Jack stared. "Seriously. Okay, that's... that's a lot."

Harper stroked Snowball's ears, laughing. "She knows where the heat is."

Jack shook his head. "No. She knows who she's picked."

Harper swallowed, her cheeks warming again.

Outside, the snowfall resumed, soft, steady, shimmering through the workshop windows like confetti from an unseen hand.

Harper typed another sentence.

Snowball purred.

Jack worked.

The world held its breath.

It was, Harper realized, the closest thing to peace she'd felt in years.

And she had absolutely no idea what it meant yet.

But she wanted to find out.

Chapter 5
Craft, Care, and a Cunning Bookseller

By late afternoon, the workshop had grown dim. The sky outside had taken on that winter shade of steel-blue that meant the sun was giving up early for the day. Harper blinked at her laptop screen, realizing with a start that she had written... several pages.

Real pages.

Not grocery lists.

Not deleted metaphors.

Pages that felt like her.

She sat back, stretching her arms overhead until her spine popped.

Jack looked up from the set of legs he was attaching to the copper-detailed table. "Good session?"

She looked at the screen again. "I think so. I don't hate any of it. That's new."

Jack smiled, that quiet, slow smile of his. "Then it's a good day."

Snowball, curled on a flannel blanket near the woodstove, opened one eye and made a soft mrrt noise, as if to say *I did more than anyone here.*

Harper laughed lightly. "Thank you for the space. Really. I think I needed... all of this." She gestured at the workshop, the warmth, him, the smell of cedar and sawdust.

Jack nodded. "It's why I built this place. I needed a space where things could take shape. No noise. No rush."

Harper tilted her head. "What made you switch from engineering to woodworking? If you don't mind me asking."

Jack paused mid-motion. Something passed over his face, a flicker of memory or loss, or both.

"I don't mind," he said finally. He set the table upright, then leaned against the bench. "I was a structural engineer for fifteen years. Big buildings. Skyscrapers. The kind that look impressive on paper." He exhaled slowly. "Then an older building I'd flagged for reinforcement collapsed after a storm. I'd pushed for repairs, but the company delayed. Budget issues. Politics." His jaw tightened. "People got hurt. One man died."

Harper felt her heart give a painful twist. "Jack... I'm so sorry."

He nodded once. "It wasn't my fault, legally. But it felt like my fault. Like I'd helped build something that could fail." He looked around the workshop. "So I came back here. Started small. Things I could hold with my hands. Things I could fix. Things that meant something to people."

Harper followed his gaze around the room: the careful craftsmanship, the warm light, the gentle hum of something healing.

"It shows," she said softly.

He met her eyes. There was a steadiness there she hadn't noticed before, a kind of weathered resilience that made her chest feel strangely warm.

Before either of them could say more, a sudden *tap-tap-tap* rattled the workshop window.

Harper jumped. Snowball hissed in protest.

Jack wiped his hands on a rag and went to the door. "I swear, if it's Tom asking me to build twenty more reindeer cut-outs for the park…"

But when he opened the door, cold air rushed in, along with Eloise Hart.

Bundled in a red coat, cheeks flushed from the cold, she bustled inside like a brisk wind in human form.

"There you two are!" she declared. "Conspiring together while the town suffers!"

Jack blinked. "Eloise, what—"

"We have a problem," she announced, thrusting a folded piece of paper into Jack's hands. "The vendor who was supposed to bring the display tables for the book fair? He's cancelled. Something about a broken axle." She waved it away. "Anyway, we need tables. Many tables. Beautiful tables. Holiday tables."

Jack opened the paper, frowning. "This is... ten tables."

"Twelve," Eloise corrected. "I forgot two on the list. Harper, dear, hello. You look radiant."

Harper blinked. "Hello. I'm... what's happening?"

"Jack is saving the book fair," Eloise said grandly, gesturing to him like a magician unveiling her assistant.

Jack looked pained. "Eloise..."

"Oh hush," she said. "You build tables in your sleep. You made that lovely bench for the community garden in an afternoon."

"That took me two weeks," Jack muttered.

"Details," Eloise said. Then she turned to Harper with a twinkling smile. "And you, my dear, are absolutely doing a reading."

Harper's stomach dropped. "What? Oh, no. No, no. I can't—"

"You must," Eloise said, undeterred. "You're a bestselling author in a town of six thousand. This is like dropping Beyoncé into a karaoke bar. You will pull in a crowd.”

Harper shook her head. “I’m barely writing anything. I’m not prepared—”

“Perfect,” Eloise said. “Authenticity sells at WinterFest. People love when authors are vulnerable and charmingly frazzled.”

“That’s not—”

“Oh, and I’ve already put your name on the posters,” Eloise added cheerfully. “They look lovely.”

Jack rubbed a hand over his face, struggling not to laugh.

Harper made a strangled sound. “You what?”

“You’ll be fine,” Eloise said, patting her arm. “You have presence. And a good hat.”

Harper stared. “My hat?”

“It suggests creative instability,” Eloise explained. “People trust that.”

Jack choked.

Snowball looked personally offended by this entire exchange.

Eloise clapped her mittened hands. “Now! Jack, can you manage twelve tables by next Friday?”

Jack opened his mouth, closed it, sighed. "Yes. I'll make it work."

"Excellent!" Eloise beamed. "And Harper, you're reading at four p.m. during the Lantern Lighting Ceremony."

"I didn't agree to—"

"Wonderful! I'll send you the program."

And with that, Eloise swept back out the door, trailing snowflakes and chaos.

The workshop fell silent.

Jack slowly turned to Harper, apology on his face. "She... means well."

Harper pressed her hands to her temples. "She put me on a poster."

Jack grinned, leaning back against his workbench. "Welcome to Cedar Hollow. Consent is more of a... suggestion here."

Harper groaned. Snowball hopped onto her lap as if to provide comfort, though her kneading claws suggested otherwise.

"You okay?" Jack asked, voice gentle.

Harper looked up at him, flustered and warm and chaotic all at once. "I... don't know," she admitted. "This is a lot."

Jack nodded. "Hey. You don't have to do it. If you want, I'll talk to Eloise. She'll understand."

Harper exhaled slowly. "No. She cares about the book fair. And the shop. And the town." Her voice softened. "And honestly... maybe it's good for me to be terrified of something that isn't my blank page."

Jack's eyes softened. "You're braver than you think."

Harper swallowed. The warmth in her chest expanded, unsettling but not unwelcome.

"Well," Jack said, picking up a pencil and lightly tapping it on the table, "if you need help practicing your reading... or someone to sit in the front row and pretend to be impressed..."

Harper smiled. "Would you?"

Jack smiled back. "In a heartbeat."

Outside, the snow continued to fall, slow, steady, quiet, the world softening under the weight of possibility.

And somewhere, Eloise Hart was no doubt pinning Harper's name to a bulletin board with the enthusiasm of someone loading a slingshot.

Chapter 6
Practices, Panic, and an Interruption

Harper spent the next morning pretending she *wasn't* panicking.

She cleaned the kitchen. Rearranged the mugs. Alphabetized Eloise's book selections (something Eloise herself would surely have forbidden). Swept the front hall. Brushed Snowball until the cat looked like a small, furious cloud.

When none of that slowed her pulse, she paced the living room, reading aloud from her manuscript.

"...and the winter wind carried the echoes of—no, that's terrible—carried the memory—also terrible—carried the... oh, for the love of cocoa."

She slumped onto the couch. Snowball leapt onto her chest like a weighted therapy device with claws.

"Eloise put me on a poster," Harper told the cat. "I'm not a performer. I'm barely a functioning writer most days."

Snowball blinked judgmentally.

Harper sighed. "I know. Adults are ridiculous."

A knock sounded at the back door.

Harper startled, nearly spilling Snowball onto the floor. She disentangled herself and crossed the kitchen, pulling open the door.

Jack stood there, bundled in his winter jacket, cheeks pink from cold, holding two travel mugs and a tote bag.

"I come bearing cocoa and bribes," he said.

Harper blinked. "Are bribes supposed to look that delicious?"

Jack grinned, handing her a mug. "Eloise told me you were practicing. Thought you might want a break."

"I've been... trying," Harper said, wrapping her hands around the warm cup.

"Trying is more than most people do," Jack said. "Mind if I come in?"

She stepped aside. "Of course not."

Jack's presence warmed the kitchen immediately, filling the space with the scent of cedar and winter air. Snowball waltzed in, rubbed once against Jack's pant leg, then disappeared, clearly leaving them to their human nonsense.

Jack looked around. "You've been cleaning."

Harper groaned. "Bad sign, right?"

"I'm not judging," he said, smiling. "I stress-built a canoe once."

Harper blinked. "A *canoe*?"

Jack shrugged. "Seemed reasonable at the time."

She laughed, tension easing a little.

He nodded toward the tote bag. "I brought something that might help."

Harper's curiosity flared. "What is it?"

Jack reached inside and pulled out... a small wooden box, polished to a soft sheen. He set it on the table and flipped the latch.

Inside lay a beautifully crafted lantern, carved with tiny stars, its panels inlaid with frosted glass.

"Oh," Harper breathed. "Jack... it's beautiful."

"I made it last year for WinterFest," he said. "Didn't get finished in time. Thought maybe... having something familiar to look at might help with the nerves tomorrow."

Harper traced a fingertip along the carved stars. "This is... perfect."

Jack met her eyes. "You will be too."

For a heartbeat, the kitchen seemed to shrink, the air thinning, warming, pulling them closer. Harper's breath caught.

He stepped back a little, clearing his throat. "If you want to practice your reading... I can listen. No pressure."

Harper hesitated, but only for a moment. He had been nothing but patient, steady, unassuming. A harbor in the storm her mind had become.

"Okay," she said softly. "But if I'm terrible, you're legally required to lie."

Jack held up a hand. "Scout's honor."

They moved into the living room. Harper stood beneath the pergola lights' reflection on the window, script in hand. Jack sat on the edge of the couch, not too close, not too far, exactly where someone sits when they want you to feel safe.

Harper inhaled and began reading.

Her voice wavered at first, thin, shaky, catching on her nerves, but the words steadied as she went. Jack nodded at the right moments, smiled at the funny ones, leaned forward during the more poignant lines.

Halfway through, Harper realized something shocking.

She wasn't just reading.

She was performing.

And she didn't hate it.

When she finally lowered the pages, heart thumping, Jack clapped once, sharply, loudly, then softened into a warm, sincere smile.

"That was wonderful."

Harper's cheeks burned. "You're being nice."

"No," Jack said. "I'm being honest. You draw people in."

Her breath hitched.

The warmth between them shifted, not casual now, not harmless. Something aware. Open. Electric.

Jack stood slowly, stepping closer. Not too close, but close enough that Harper felt his presence like a temperature.

"Harper…"

The way he said her name made something inside her tighten.

She opened her mouth, to say what, she didn't know, when a sharp *crash* erupted from the kitchen.

Both of them jumped.

"Snowball!" Harper yelped, rushing in.

Snowball sat on the counter, smugly beside an overturned jar of cat treats, one paw resting on a single fallen treat like a pirate claiming treasure.

Jack laughed helplessly in the doorway. "She has the timing of a seasoned chaperone."

Harper scooped Snowball into her arms. "You little saboteur!"

Snowball purred loudly. Jack leaned in, brushing a finger over the cat's head.

"Guess the universe isn't ready for whatever *that* almost was," he murmured.

Harper swallowed, pulse fluttering.

"Maybe it's waiting for the right moment," she said softly.

Jack's eyes warmed. "Maybe."

Snowball wriggled out of her arms, triumphant.

Harper exhaled shakily. "Well... that was almost something."

Jack nodded. "Almost."

And there it was again, that electricity that hovered between almost and not-yet.

Outside the window, tiny flakes began to fall, swirling past the glass like a promise.

Chapter 7
Lanterns and Laughter

WinterFest began the way all Cedar Hollow events apparently began:

With music, muffins, and mild disorder.

By noon, the town square was alive with activity. Vendor tents lined the sidewalks, decorated with garlands and twinkling lights. Children in knit hats chased each other between snowbanks. The air smelled of cinnamon pastries, pine boughs, and something that might have been mulled cider, though Harper suspected Mayor Bennett had spiked it.

Harper stepped into the square feeling like someone walking into a dream with a slightly-too-real sense of responsibility.

Eloise had insisted she arrive early, "to acclimate," she'd said, though Harper suspected it was really to stop her from fleeing back to New York, and now Harper stood beside a table draped in red velvet, stacked with copies of her books.

Her name was on a banner above it.

A very large banner.

"Oh no," Harper whispered. "She used the headshot where I look like I'm thinking about overthrowing a government."

"It's a great photo," Jack said, stepping up beside her.

Harper startled, just a little, then felt the now-familiar warmth of him settle the air around her.

He looked different today. Not dramatically, but enough that she noticed. His dark jacket was replaced by a heavier wool coat, dusted with snow. His scarf was old but soft-looking. And his eyes... they were watching her with a quiet, steady encouragement that made her feel less like a woman on the verge of stage fright and more like someone capable of doing this.

"You clean up nicely," Harper said, before she could stop herself.

Jack grinned. "You don't look panicked yet. Promising start."

"Give it time," Harper said. "We're not at the reading portion."

Jack's smile softened. "You'll be great."

"I don't know that."

"I do."

She swallowed. "How?"

He shrugged slightly. "You read to me yesterday. And I wanted more."

Her pulse did something unhelpfully fluttery. "Jack…"

But before anything else could be said, Eloise materialized like a festive apparition.

"Harper! Jack! Marvelous timing. Harper, dear, you're on the program at four, but you'll want to mingle a bit. Smile. Say things like 'So good to meet you!' and 'Yes, I do drink too much coffee.' It humanizes you."

Harper stared. "Does it?"

"Oh yes. Very relatable." Eloise adjusted Harper's scarf without asking. "Jack, darling, are the tables ready?"

"Finished last night," Jack said. "Tom and I set them out this morning."

Eloise beamed at him as if he'd carved an ice sculpture with his bare hands. "Perfect! Harper, do not fret. Everyone here loves stories."

Harper nodded, though her palms were damp inside her gloves.

Eloise bustled off, presumably to orchestrate more chaos.

Jack turned back to Harper. "Want to walk around a bit before the crowd gets bigger?"

She nodded gratefully. "Yes. Please."

They wandered past booths selling knitted hats, handmade soaps, jars of spiced jam, maple candy shaped like stars. Snow fell in tiny, glittering flakes, the kind that looked like movie snow rather than the wet, slushy variety that assaulted New York sidewalks.

The town band played from a small stage, brass instruments shining under strings of lights. People waved at Jack, everyone waved at Jack, and he waved back with easy familiarity.

"He's going to be mayor one day!" someone called from a donut stall.

Jack groaned quietly. "Ignore them."

Harper grinned. "I'm not sure I can. There's a trend emerging here."

He shook his head. "I'm not running for anything. I fix tables, mend fences, and help cats negotiate emotional boundaries."

"And save bookstores," Harper added.

Jack's expression shifted, softer. "I just help where I can."

She studied him for a moment, the way he moved through the world, grounded and gentle. Not trying to impress anyone. Not performing. Just... being.

It was unsettlingly attractive.

They stopped near a booth where children decorated paper lanterns for the evening's ceremony. One lantern, abandoned mid-project, was painted with crooked stars and streaks of silver.

"You doing one?" Jack asked.

Harper made a face. "I have no artistic skill unless words count."

"They do." Jack picked up a blank lantern and a brush. "But you should try anyway."

Harper took the brush reluctantly, dipped it into pale blue paint, and stared at the empty panel.

"Okay," she said. "But don't laugh."

"I would never," Jack said solemnly.

"Liar."

"Only about muffins. This? Never."

Harper bit her lip and painted a small spiral. Then another. And another. The brush moved more easily than she'd expected. When she stepped back, the panel was covered in swirling, overlapping snowy spirals, simple, imperfect, soft.

"Oh," she said. "That's... not hideous."

"It's lovely," Jack said.

"Don't patronize me."

"I'm not." He leaned in a little. "It looks like snow caught in wind. Quiet but alive."

Harper blinked. "Jack..."

But before anything else could happen, before the moment could deepen into something undeniably charged, a familiar voice boomed behind them.

"Harper! Harper, darling, there you are!"

Eloise, waving both arms, marched toward them with the determined energy of a general.

"Quickly, dear, the local paper wants your photo! And Jack, stand with her, handsome men increase community engagement!"

Jack sighed. "Eloise..."

Harper laughed helplessly as Eloise herded them together.

"Smile!" Eloise commanded.

Harper and Jack stood shoulder to shoulder, lanterns in hand, snow falling softly around them as the photographer snapped a picture.

"Look at that," Eloise cooed. "You two photograph beautifully together."

Harper's cheeks warmed. Jack's ears turned slightly pink.

Snowball, who had appeared from *somewhere*, wound between Harper's feet and yowled disapprovingly at the photographer.

"She hates cameras," Jack said.

"She hates competition," Harper corrected.

A ripple of laughter spread from a nearby booth.

As the afternoon wore on, Harper found herself relaxing. People approached her shyly, asking about her books, telling her which characters they loved, sharing stories of how reading had gotten them through long winters or hard years.

Harper listened, humbled. Touched. Something she thought she'd lost, connection, presence, returned in small, flickering pieces.

Through it all, Jack stayed nearby. Not hovering. Just there. A steady presence in a sea of faces.

By the time the sky began to dim toward evening, Harper's chest felt full, in a way that wasn't frightening, for once.

It felt like belonging.

And yet... her reading was still ahead. The thought fluttered uncomfortably in her stomach.

Jack noticed.

He stepped closer, lowering his voice. "When you go up there, just find one face in the crowd. Someone who makes you feel steady. And read to them. No one else."

Harper swallowed. "Who would that be?"

He held her gaze.

"You already know," he said quietly.

Her pulse stumbled.

But before she could answer, the lanterns began to glow across the square, hundreds of tiny, flickering lights rising like captured stars.

It was time.

Chapter 8
The Reading and Lanterns

Twilight settled over Cedar Hollow like a velvet blanket.

As the last of the afternoon light faded, lanterns flickered awake across the town square—soft yellows, pale blues, warm reds—each one painted by small hands, careful hands, hands that believed in the simple magic of light against dark.

A small wooden stage had been set up near the fountain, decorated with evergreen boughs and strings of white lights. Eloise hovered near the podium like a proud stage mother moments before a recital.

Harper's stomach performed a slow, complicated flip.

People were gathering—families with steaming cups of cider, teenagers wrapped in scarves, older couples leaning into each other. Children darted between legs, waving lanterns like fireflies.

Jack touched her elbow gently.

"You ready?"

Harper swallowed. "Define ready."

Jack smiled softly. "Breathing counts."

She exhaled shakily. "Barely."

"You'll be wonderful," he said. His voice was low, near enough that it brushed the side of her neck like warmth. "Just remember—find one face."

Her breath caught. "Yours?"

Jack didn't hesitate. "If you want."

Something inside her faltered and steadied all at once.

"Yes," she whispered. "Yours."

Eloise clapped sharply. "Harper! Places!"

Jack nudged her forward. "Go get 'em."

Harper climbed the three wooden steps to the stage. Her boots felt heavier than they should. Her hands trembled as she took her place behind the podium.

The crowd quieted gradually, lantern lights shimmering across a sea of expectant faces.

Harper cleared her throat. The microphone crackled.

"I, uh... I'm Harper Lane," she said.

"Some of you know me from my books... and some of you know me because Eloise may or may not have threatened to disown anyone who didn't show up tonight."

A ripple of laughter moved through the square. Harper felt something ease in her chest.

She glanced up—straight at Jack.

He stood just off-center, hands in his pockets, face open and steady. The lantern light caught the flecks of copper in his eyes.

She inhaled deeply and began.

The passage she chose wasn't dramatic. Not her most clever. Not her most intense. It was a quiet scene—two characters in one of her earlier books sitting together after a storm, admitting small truths.

Harper had always liked it because it felt... honest. Human.

As she read, her voice found rhythm. Warmth. Cadence.

She forgot the crowd. Forgot the banner with her face.

Forgot her fear.

She read to Jack—only Jack.

but too short to be a decision—

Jack stepped back half a pace.

Harper blinked. "Wait—"

He shook his head gently. "Not here. Not... like this. You're overwhelmed. You deserve a moment that isn't pulled from under your feet."

Her heart stuttered.

He wasn't rejecting her.

He was waiting.

Choosing the right moment.

She swallowed hard. "I'm not afraid."

"I know," he said softly. "But I want the first time I kiss you to be when you're not shaking from adrenaline."

Her breath escaped in a soft, unsteady laugh.

Snowball trotted up at that exact instant, tail curled, as if checking the perimeter for scandal.

Jack exhaled, tension easing. "See? Even the cat thinks we need supervision."

Harper knelt and rubbed Snowball's head, mostly to keep from leaning right into Jack again.

Snowball blinked sagely.

And Harper thought:

I'm in trouble.

The good kind.

The kind she didn't know she'd been waiting for.

The kind she wasn't sure she wanted to stop.

Chapter 9
Echoes of an Unexpected Call

Harper barely remembered the rest of the evening.

She remembered lanterns rising into the deepening dusk—soft orbs floating upward on gentle currents of warm air. She remembered people hugging her, shaking her hand, thanking her for words she almost hadn't written. She remembered cocoa and laughter and the glow of WinterFest curling around her like a story being told back to her.

But mostly... she remembered Jack.

The way he'd looked at her after the reading.

The way he'd stepped back with a tenderness she hadn't expected.

The way his voice had dropped when he said *I want the first time I kiss you to be different.*

Walking home, lanterns bobbing behind them, Harper felt her pulse in every layer of clothing.

Jack didn't say much. He didn't need to. His presence was enough—steadily matching her steps, offering his hand when the sidewalk grew slick, letting their fingers brush once, twice, three times...

Each brush was a spark.

At her front steps, Harper fumbled with her keys, cheeks burning from the cold *and* from everything unspoken between them.

"Thank you," she said softly. "For... everything. Today. The workshop. The practice. Being there."

Jack's gaze held hers. Quiet. Warm. A little unreadable.

"Anytime," he murmured.

Snowball flopped dramatically against the door, as if announcing she was freezing to death and required immediate access to her throne.

Harper laughed, breaking the tension, and opened the door.

Jack lingered on the step.

"Goodnight, Harper," he said, voice low.

She swallowed. "Goodnight."

And then he walked back toward his place, hands in pockets, lantern light catching on the snow at his boots.

Harper closed the door behind her and leaned against it, heart pounding in every direction.

Snowball trotted into the living room, tail twitching. Harper followed, dropping her coat on the couch.

"You," she told the cat. "Are a menace to romance."

Snowball hopped onto the armchair and rolled onto her side with deliberate insolence.

Harper smiled helplessly, sinking onto the couch and rubbing her hands over her face.

She didn't know what this was.

She didn't know where it was going.

She only knew she hadn't felt this alive in years.

The knock on the door startled her.

Harper jumped up, heart leaping. Jack? Had he come back? Had he changed his mind? Had he—

She opened the door.

It wasn't Jack.

It was her phone buzzing in her hand.

Mara calling.

At 10:14 p.m.

Harper hesitated, thumb hovering. Mara wouldn't call this late unless something was urgent.

She answered. "Hey. Is everything okay?"

There was a beat of silence.

Then Mara's voice—too calm. Too careful.

"Harper... I've been trying to reach you earlier, but the reception out there is impossible."

Harper's stomach dipped. "What's wrong?"

Mara exhaled softly. "The publisher moved up the deadline."

Harper closed her eyes. "Mara..."

"They want a completed manuscript by January fifth," Mara said quickly. "Or they'll pass the contract to another author. And, Harper... they're serious. They need something to anchor next year's lineup."

Harper felt the warmth drain from her limbs.

January fifth.

That was less than three weeks away.

"I'm just getting started," Harper whispered. "I've barely found my footing again."

"I know," Mara said gently. "I *know*. And your pages so far—Harper, they're good. Better than good. You've got something here. But you need time. And they're not giving it."

Her heartbeat thudded in her ears.

"So what are you saying?"

"I'm saying," Mara said softly, "you may have to come back to New York."

The words hit like cold water.

The house around her—the warmth, the quiet, the smell of pine and old wood—suddenly felt fragile.

Temporary.

Harper swallowed hard. "Mara... I'm not ready."

"I know," her friend repeated. "But we have to be realistic."

Harper stared at her reflection in the dark window. Lanterns glowed outside. Snow fell gently past the pergola lights.

And in the distance, a silhouette moved from Jack's workshop back toward his house—tired, steady, unaware that Harper's world had just tilted.

"Harper?" Mara's voice was soft. "Talk to me."

Harper forced her voice steady. "I'll... I'll call you tomorrow. I need to think."

"Okay," Mara said. "I'm here when you're ready."

The call ended.

Silence rushed in.

Snowball leapt onto the couch and head-butted Harper's arm. Harper stroked the cat absently, staring out at the falling snow.

She had finally found words again.

Found peace again.

Found... something she wasn't ready to name.

And now?

It felt like sand slipping through her fingers.

Harper whispered into the quiet:

"What am I going to do?"

Snowball answered with a soft, insistent mrrp—as if the answers were obvious, if only Harper were willing to see them.

Tomorrow, she'd have to face Jack.

Tomorrow, she'd have to face herself.

Tonight, she sat in the falling snow's glow, heart aching with something that was both hope and fear.

Something that felt far too much like love.

Chapter 10

Cracks in the Quiet

Harper didn't sleep. She drifted in and out of restless half-dreams—snow swirling, pages tearing, city lights flickering far away, Jack's voice saying her name like a promise she couldn't keep.

By morning, her pillow was cold and she felt hollow in a way that didn't match the softness of Cedar Hollow at all.

Snowball kneaded her ribs pointedly, demanding breakfast and emotional stability.

Harper fed her both as best she could.

She lingered over coffee, staring at the steam curling upward, thinking about everything and nothing—her deadline, her stalled career, the pages she'd begun to love again, the town she'd unexpectedly fallen for, the man who made her feel seen.

And then the knock came.

Soft. Three raps. Familiar.

Her heart stumbled.

She opened the door.

Jack stood there in a navy sweater and wool coat, snow in his hair, concern in his eyes.

"You weren't at the workshop," he said.

Harper swallowed. "I... I needed a morning."

Jack studied her for a moment, brows drawing together. "Everything okay?"

No.

Yes.

Maybe.

Absolutely not.

She managed a thin smile. "Just tired."

He stepped closer—not touching her, but close enough that the warmth of him cut through the cold air drifting in from outside.

"You can tell me," he said quietly. "If something happened."

His voice—gentle, steady, so painfully kind—made her throat tighten.

Harper looked down. "It's nothing you can fix."

Jack hesitated, then tipped his head a fraction, catching her gaze again.

"That doesn't mean I don't want to know."

Harper's breath wavered.

This was the danger.

This tenderness.

This pull.

She stepped back and gestured him inside. Jack wiped snow from his boots and entered, eyes tracking her with quiet worry.

Snowball strutted forward like a monarch inspecting her subjects. Jack bent down and rubbed her head.

"At least *someone* is happy to see me," he murmured.

Harper huffed a weak laugh. "She's selective."

Jack straightened again. "Harper... what's wrong?"

She crossed her arms without meaning to—a shield against a truth that terrified her.

"I got a call from Mara last night," she said softly.

Jack nodded slowly. "The friend you mentioned. Your editor."

"Yeah." Harper swallowed. "The publisher... moved up my deadline. To January fifth."

Jack blinked. "That's... soon."

"Very," Harper whispered. "Too soon."

She wrapped her arms tighter around herself.

"If I don't go back to New York, there's no way I make the deadline. And if I miss it... they're done with me. I lose the contract. I lose... everything."

Jack exhaled—a heavy, pained sound.

"You just got here," he said quietly.

"I know." Her voice cracked. "And I just... started writing again. For the first time in months. And it's because of this place. And you. And Snowball." She laughed shakily. "But I can't stay and magically produce a book. It doesn't work that way."

Jack stepped closer, slowly, like approaching a skittish deer. "Harper..."

She shook her head. "I can't ask you—or this town—for more than what I've already taken. I came here to breathe, not to build a life I can't keep."

Jack's eyes softened with something that hurt to look at.

Something about loss.

Something about wanting more.

"You think staying would be taking?" he asked, voice barely above a whisper.

Harper froze.

"I think staying would be selfish," she whispered back.

He looked at her for a long, quiet moment.

Then he shook his head.

"That's the first thing you've said that I can't agree with."

Harper blinked, breath catching.

"You haven't taken anything," Jack said gently. "You've given. You don't even see it, but you have. To the bookshop. To WinterFest. To... me."

Her heart tripped.

He looked down, breath moving slow and uneven. "I didn't realize how quiet my life had gotten until you showed up. And suddenly, the silence didn't feel comforting anymore. It felt... incomplete."

Harper's throat tightened painfully.

"Jack..." she whispered.

He looked up, eyes soft, vulnerable. "You haven't been selfish. Not once."

Harper blinked rapidly. Tears she didn't want, didn't expect, stung her eyes.

"I don't want to leave," she whispered.

"I don't want you to leave," he answered.

Snowball hopped onto the arm of the couch with impeccable timing, meowing loudly—judging them both for their emotional incompetence.

Harper let out a wet laugh. Jack smiled weakly.

But the moment hung there—fragile, heavy, electric.

"What do you want to do?" Jack asked.

"I don't know," Harper said honestly. "If I stay, I risk everything. If I go... I lose everything that matters here."

Jack stepped forward—very slow, very gentle.

He didn't touch her.

He didn't have to.

"You don't have to decide today," he murmured. "You don't have to decide alone."

Her breath hitched. "Jack..."

He exhaled, something like hope flickering behind his eyes.

"I'm here," he said softly. "Whatever you choose."

Harper looked up at him. Really looked—at the steadiness, the patience, the way he held space for her fear without demanding she erase it.

Something inside her cracked open.

Not breaking—

opening.

And the cold Cedar Hollow morning suddenly felt warmer than any sunlit day she'd had in New York.

Chapter 11
The Offer, the Idea, the Bookshop

Harper tried to work that afternoon, but the words wouldn't come.

She sat at the table, laptop open, Snowball curled in a loaf-shape beside her—judging her productivity with half-lidded disdain.

A paragraph.

Delete.

Three sentences.

Delete.

One line.

Stare at it until it withered into self-consciousness. Delete.

Snowball flicked her tail sharply.

"I know," Harper muttered. "Unproductive. Borderline tragic."

Snowball kneaded her sleeve once—perhaps encouragement, perhaps punishment.

Harper closed the laptop and rubbed her temples.

Her thoughts churned like snow in a wind gust:

Going back to New York.

Leaving Cedar Hollow.
Losing the book.

Losing Jack.

Losing herself again in the noise.

A knock startled her.

When she opened the door, Jack stood there holding two paper bags and wearing an expression halfway between worry and stubborn resolve.

"I brought lunch," he said. "And a stupid idea."

Harper blinked. "Well. I'm intrigued already."

He stepped inside, brushing snow from his shoulders. He set the bags on the table—soup from the café, warm bread, and something that smelled suspiciously like Eloise's cookies.

Jack tugged off his gloves. "Okay. So. The idea. And keep in mind, you're allowed to tell me it's terrible."

"Noted."

He met her eyes. "What if you didn't have to go back to New York to write?"

Harper's breath caught. "Jack—"

"No, hear me out. You've done more writing here in a week than you did in months there. You're focused. You're steady. The environment works."

"Jack, the editor needs me physically present. Meetings. Rewrites. Promo shooting. It's a whole circus."

Jack nodded. "Then... what only needs you on Zoom?"

Harper blinked.

Zoom.

"Jack," she said slowly, "my publisher doesn't exactly encourage remote work."

"Do they forbid it?"

"...no."

He spread his hands like the answer was obvious. "Then call Mara. Ask. The worst they can say is no."

Harper stared at him. "Jack, you're talking about changing how an entire publishing house works."

"I'm talking about giving you the chance to keep breathing," Jack corrected gently.

Her throat tightened.

"I know," he continued, "that what happens next is your call. Your career. Your future. Your fight. But you don't have to fight it alone."

Snowball leapt onto the table, as if to say *I will also be providing moral support.*

Harper choked on a laugh. "You two make a formidable team."

Jack smiled softly. "We like to think so."

Something warm blossomed in her chest—hope, fragile but real.

But before she could respond, Snowball suddenly jumped off the table and trotted to the front window, tail straight up.

She chirped.

Harper frowned. "Is that...?"

A knock rattled the front door.

Before Harper even reached it, Eloise let herself in.

Because Eloise was Eloise.

"Harper, dear! I brought something terribly dangerous!"

She held up a folder stuffed with papers.

Jack groaned. "Eloise—"

"Not you, darling. You're perfect." She patted his arm, then thrust the folder at Harper like a weapon.

Harper opened it.

Inside were—

"No way," she breathed.

—signed WinterFest programs with *her* name highlighted in gold

—two printed articles about *her* reading, including a glowing piece from the local paper

—photos of Harper on stage

—and a flyer mockup that read:

UPCOMING AUTHOR SERIES
Featuring Harper Lane

Harper looked up, stunned. "Eloise... what is this?"

"A marketing packet," Eloise said proudly. "Publishers adore these."

Jack blinked. "You... made her a press kit?"

"Of course I did," Eloise sniffed. "Harper is a treasure and I refuse to let any big-city operation treat her like an afterthought."

Harper stared between them, throat tightening. "Eloise... I can't ask you to—"

"You didn't ask," Eloise said, patting her cheek. "I'm doing it because I care. And because I want to keep my bookshop. And because Cedar Hollow desperately needs an author-in-residence who wears nice hats."

Jack tried not to laugh.

Eloise leaned in. "Call your editor. Send her this. Tell her you're thriving out here and can finish the manuscript if she gives you room to breathe."

Harper felt her knees weaken.

"I—" She stood there, swallowed hard. "I don't know what to say."

Eloise placed her hands on Harper's shoulders, eyes bright and fierce behind her glasses.

"Say yes," she whispered. "To the thing you want."

Harper froze.

Because she suddenly knew Eloise wasn't talking about the manuscript.

Jack shifted slightly behind her, and the air seemed to warm.

Eloise clapped her hands, startling both of them. "Wonderful! I'll leave you two to conspire. Snowball, dear, your fur is immaculate today."

Snowball chirped smugly.

And Eloise swept out the door, trailing pine-scented chaos behind her.

Harper turned back to Jack, who raised his eyebrows. "See? I'm not the only one who thinks you deserve better than panic and deadlines."

Harper's pulse fluttered. "Jack... I'm scared."

He nodded. "Good. Scared means it matters."

Her eyes stung again.

She hated how often that was happening here.

She also didn't hate it at all.

"What if Mara says no?" she whispered.

"Then you go," Jack said softly. "And you finish the book. And you succeed. And when you're done... I'll still be here."

Her breath caught. "Jack..."

He stepped closer, slow and steady, like he always moved with her.

"You won't lose me," he said quietly. "Not because of a job. Not because of distance. Not because you're trying to build a life you fought hard for."

Harper couldn't speak. The world softened around her, like snow falling in slow motion.

Jack exhaled through a faint smile. "And if she says yes?"

Harper whispered, "Then I stay."

Jack's eyes warmed with a hope so gentle it hurt to look at.

"Then you stay," he echoed.

And for the first time since the phone call...

Harper felt possibility.

Real possibility.

She looked down at the press kit, then at Snowball, then at Jack.

"I'll call Mara," she said finally. "Tonight."

Jack nodded. "I'll be here."

And somehow, Harper knew he meant it.

Chapter 12
The Call and the Wait

Harper paced the living room like it was a hallway outside an operating room.

Snowball followed in tight circles, clearly annoyed that the human had chosen *walking in anxious loops* over *providing snacks*. The winter evening pressed softly against the windows, the pergola lights glowing like a constellation that had chosen this backyard specifically.

Jack had gone home to "give you space," as he put it, though he'd said it in a tone that implied *I'll only be twenty steps away if you need me.*

Harper checked her phone.

No missed messages.

No updates.

Just the weight of a phone call she'd been putting off for hours.

She took a breath, steeled herself, and pressed **Mara — Call**.

It rang once.

Twice.

Then—

"Harper? Thank god. I was staring at my inbox like a Victorian widow."

Harper exhaled a shaky laugh. "Hi."

"You sound like someone about to confess to a crime," Mara said. "What happened?"

Harper sat, curling her legs beneath her. Snowball hopped onto her lap, heavy with authority.

"I want to stay in Cedar Hollow," Harper said, voice trembling. "I'm writing again here. I'm... breathing again here."

Mara didn't respond right away.

"Mara?" Harper asked, heart pounding.

"I'm here," Mara said. Her voice had softened. "Harper... good. That's good. That's *very* good. But what about the timeline?"

"I think I can finish," Harper said. "If I can work remotely. If I'm not forced back into the same chaos."

"Remote," Mara repeated slowly. "The big execs aren't fans."

"But is it impossible?" Harper whispered.

Another pause.

The kind that contained calculations, negotiations, and the subtle sound of Mara pacing her Brooklyn apartment.

"It's not impossible," Mara said at last. "But it's not automatic, either. They need a reason strong enough to bend the rule."

Harper's chest tightened. "I can send the press kit Eloise put together."

"Eloise?" Mara echoed.

"The bookseller here. She's..." Harper swallowed. "She's an entire force of nature."

"Sounds dangerous. I like her already," Mara murmured. "Okay. Press kit, fine. But the real question is—can you finish this book on time?"

Harper looked at the workshop lantern Jack made.

At Snowball grooming her paw.

At the snow falling past the window.

"Yes," Harper said, voice steady. "I can finish it here."

"Then I'll fight for you," Mara said simply. "But Harper... you need to be prepared."

"For what?"

"For them to say no," Mara said gently. "And for you to decide what you want even if they don't bend."

Harper's heart squeezed. "I know."

Mara hesitated. "Harper... can I ask you something personal?"

"Sure."

"Did something change out there?" Mara asked. "Besides the writing?"

Harper froze.

Snowball paused mid-lick, ears twitching.

"What do you mean?" Harper said too quickly.

"Your voice," Mara said. "There's... something in it. Like hope, but also like terror."

Harper closed her eyes. "There's someone here."

Mara made a soft, knowing sound. "Oh. Ohhh."

"Mara—"

"No, no, I'm thrilled for you," Mara said. "But Harper... don't let the idea of a man derail your career. Even if he's handsome. Even if he's kind. Even if he smells like pine and emotional stability."

Harper laughed helplessly. "It's not about Jack. It's about... me. About where I can actually write."

"Then we push," Mara said. "We push until they agree. Or we walk and publish somewhere that treats you like a human."

Harper blinked hard. "Mara..."

"I said I'd fight for you," Mara reminded her. "I meant it."

Harper felt warmth bloom in her chest. Gratitude. Relief. Fierce love for her stubborn friend.

"Send me the materials," Mara said. "I'll call you first thing in the morning after I talk to them."

"Okay."

"And Harper?"

"Yeah?"

"If staying in Cedar Hollow makes you a better version of yourself... then stay. The rest is logistics."

Harper swallowed tightly. "Thank you."

"Go write," Mara said. "Go breathe."

The call ended.

Harper sat there, staring at Snowball.

Snowball blinked.

"I think," Harper whispered, "something is shifting."

Snowball chirped, clearly meaning *Finally*.

As Harper stood, gathering the press kit and her notes, a sound drifted from outside—

A quiet thud.

Footsteps on fresh snow.

Jack.

Her heart leapt before she could stop it.

She opened the door.

He stood there, breath clouding in the cold, scarf dusted in flakes. A single lantern glow reflected in his eyes.

"How'd it go?" he asked gently.

Harper didn't speak.

Not yet.

She stepped forward.

Jack's breath hitched.

"I might get to stay," she whispered, voice trembling with hope. "I don't know yet. But... I might."

Jack exhaled slowly, like he'd been holding that breath since yesterday.

His voice was soft. Unsteady.

"Harper..."

She took one step closer.

Jack's hands lifted—hesitating—then gently cupped her face, thumbs brushing the cold from her cheeks.

Her breath shivered.

"I ran out of reasons not to do this," he murmured.

And then he kissed her.

It wasn't rushed.

It wasn't tentative.

It was warm, and certain, and full of the quiet promise he'd been holding back since the moment she arrived.

Harper melted into him, fingers curling into his coat.

The snow fell around them like confetti.

Snowball meowed from inside, scandalized but approving.

When they finally parted, Harper's voice was a whisper:

"What happens now?"

Jack rested his forehead against hers.

"Now?" he said softly. "We hope for good news. And if it doesn't come... we find another way."

Harper closed her eyes.

For the first time in a long time—

Hope didn't feel like a risk.

It felt like a home.

Chapter 13

The Answer and the Storm

arper woke before dawn, long before the weak winter light brushed the horizon.

She lay still beneath the quilt, listening to the hush of snowflakes brushing the windows.

Today was the day Mara would call.

Today was the day everything might shift—forward or backward, open or closed.

Snowball sprawled across Harper's feet, purring with the deep, self-satisfied confidence of someone who believed the universe obeyed her.

"Mara better call soon," Harper whispered. "I'm not built for suspense."

Snowball thumped her tail in agreement—or impatience.

Just after eight, Harper's phone buzzed.

Her stomach plummeted.

Her pulse stuttered.

She answered. "Mara?"

Mara exhaled on the other end. It wasn't a good exhale. It wasn't a triumphant one either. It was the kind someone gives when they've been fighting for hours.

"Okay," Mara said. "I've talked to everyone. Your editor. Their boss. Their boss's boss. Their boss's assistant who doesn't get paid enough to care but weirdly does. And... we got them halfway."

Harper's breath snagged. "Halfway?"

"Yes," Mara said. "They're willing to let you stay in Cedar Hollow *if*—and Harper, this is a very big if—you can get them a full, polished draft by January second."

Harper closed her eyes.

"That's three days earlier."

"I know," Mara said. "But it was the only compromise they were willing to budge on."

Silence pressed between them—cold, tight, trembling.

Harper forced her voice steady. "Can I do it?"

"Harper..." Mara exhaled. "You're brilliant. But it won't be easy. You'll have to live inside that manuscript. No breaks. No second-guessing. No perfectionism. Just writing."

Harper's pulse hammered. "And if I fail?"

"They'll terminate the contract," Mara said. "And they'll hold your next advance against you."

Harper closed her eyes. "So either I leave or I push harder than I've ever pushed."

"Pretty much," Mara said. Then softly: "If it helps... I believe you can."

Harper breathed slowly. "Okay."

"Okay?"

"Okay," Harper repeated, firmer this time. "I'll try."

"That's all I needed to hear." Mara paused. "And Harper?"

"Yeah?"

"You sound alive again. Don't lose that, whatever happens."

The call ended.

Harper sat very still.

Snowball climbed into her lap, purring louder—as if to say *You didn't ask my opinion, but I approve.*

A soft knock sounded at the door.

Harper opened it to find Jack, hair tousled, snow in his eyelashes, concern in every line of his posture.

"You heard?" Harper asked.

He nodded. "You okay?"

Harper exhaled. "They'll let me stay... if I finish the book early. January second."

Jack processed that, jaw tightening with a mix of anger and protectiveness. "That's... impossible."

Harper looked up at him. "I've done impossible things before."

He studied her face. "Do you want to try?"

She swallowed. "Yes."

Something in his expression shifted—respect, pride, tenderness.

Something fiercer than either of them expected.

"Then we make it possible," Jack said.

Harper blinked. "We?"

Jack stepped inside and closed the door gently behind him.

"I'm not letting you go through this alone," he said simply. "I'll bring meals. I'll keep the house quiet. I'll keep Snowball from staging coups. I'll read if you want. Or sit nearby while you write. Or just... be here."

Her eyes stung. "Jack..."

He stepped closer. "Harper Lane, you have spent too many years fighting your battles alone. Not this time."

A tear slipped down her cheek. Jack brushed it away with his thumb—slow, reverent.

"That's not the only thing," he added quietly.

Harper held her breath. "What?"

Jack reached into his coat and pulled out a small wooden object.

A key.

Hand-carved. Smooth. Warm from his pocket.

Harper stared. "Jack...?"

"I told you I'd only kiss you when the moment wasn't going to be pulled out from under you," he said softly. "I meant it. But I also meant something else."

He placed the key gently in her palm.

"It's a key to the workshop," he said. "For when the house is too quiet. Or too loud. Or too cold. Or too lonely. For when you need light. Or space. Or someone to sit nearby."

Harper's throat closed. "Jack, I can't—"

"You can," he murmured. "I want you to."

Snowball meowed loudly, as if officiating.

Harper laughed through a tear. "This is... a lot."

Jack cupped her cheek again, thumb brushing softly. "So is falling for someone."

Her breath caught sharply. "Jack..."

"I'm not asking you to choose me over your work," he said. "I'm asking you to let me stay beside you while you fight for it."

Harper's heart clenched—pain and joy tangled together.

"I don't know what will happen," she whispered.

"I do," Jack said, lifting her chin gently. "You'll write. You'll try. You'll push. And I'll be here—every step."

The warmth between them thickened, deepened, pulsed with something inevitable.

Snow fell outside, silent and steady.

Harper stepped closer—so close their breath mingled, warm against the cold.

"Jack," she whispered. "Kiss me again."

His breath hitched.

"Harper—some moments aren't meant to be perfect. They're meant to be real."

And then he kissed her—

deep and slow and certain—

a kiss that tasted like winter and hope and the beginning of something impossible to deny.

When they finally parted, foreheads touching, breath unsteady, Harper murmured:

"If I'm going to finish this book... I need everything here exactly as it is."

Jack smiled, soft and fierce all at once. "Harper Lane, I promise you—Cedar Hollow will hold the line."

Chapter 14
The Push and the Hearth

Harper wrote.

She *wrote*. She wrote until her fingers ached and her eyes blurred and her coffee went cold twice before she remembered she'd made it. She wrote as if the story had been trapped under ice and Cedar Hollow had finally cracked the surface.

Word after word, scene after scene, her characters unfurled like breath in winter air.

Jack noticed the shift immediately.

He'd knock three times—always three—before letting himself into the workshop or the house. He brought soup, sandwiches, thermoses of cocoa, tea in mismatched mugs. He shooed Snowball off the keyboard with stern negotiations. He left notes:

Keep going. You're doing it.

Proud of you.

Take a break or I will physically steal your laptop.

Seriously. Hydrate.

He didn't hover. He didn't distract.

He anchored.

Snowball, meanwhile, became a tiny productivity monster. She sat on Harper's lap like a weighted blanket. She glared if Harper slowed down. She thumped her tail disapprovingly when Harper hesitated over a sentence. She was, as Jack said one evening, *"an emotionally manipulative writing coach."*

Harper wrote in the house sometimes.

In the workshop other times—especially when the silence felt too thick or the heater wheezed ominously. Jack had cleared a permanent space for her on his big worktable, complete with a soft lamp and a blanket she pretended not to use.

Word count climbed.

Scenes poured.

Her heart—terrified and thrilled—kept pace.

Every night, she fell asleep reading over what she'd written.

Every morning, she woke up eager—actually eager—to write more.

But the storm was coming.

Not weather—though snow fell constantly now, blanketing Cedar Hollow in soft white silence.

No, the storm was the deadline.

And it loomed like a winter cliff.

Three days before January second, Harper hit **the wall**.

The hard one.

The one writers pretend doesn't exist but secretly dread.

She sat in the workshop, staring at a chapter that refused to cooperate. The characters had stiffened. The dialogue clunked. The pacing collapsed like a bad soufflé.

Her breath shook.

"I can't do it," she whispered.

Snowball, offended, placed a paw on her wrist like *You can, and I demand that you do.*

Harper pressed her hands to her face. "I'm going to fail. I'm going to blow the one shot I have left. Mara is going to kill me. The publisher is going to blacklist me. I'm going to have to move back to the city and live with a roommate who eats fish in the microwave—"

The workshop door opened.

Jack stepped inside quietly. Snow dusted his shoulders. His eyes went straight to her.

"Hey," he said gently. "Talk to me."

Harper shook her head. "I'm stuck. Completely stuck. And I don't have time to be stuck."

Jack crossed the room, slow and steady. He didn't try to read the screen. He didn't flinch at the panic vibrating off her.

He simply knelt in front of her chair and rested his hands lightly on her knees.

Her breath hiccuped.

"Harper," he said softly, "you don't have to be perfect right now. You just have to keep going."

"I can't," she choked. "I'm a fraud. I'm going to let everyone down."

Jack shook his head. "You're not a fraud. You're a writer in the middle of the hardest part. You're exhausted. You're scared. But you're not done."

Her eyes stung. "Jack—"

He squeezed her knees gently. "Look at what you've written in the last week. Look at how far you've come. You didn't find your voice here—you *remembered* it."

Her throat tightened painfully.

"And you're not alone anymore," Jack whispered. "You don't have to hold this by yourself."

Her breath shuddered. He stood, lifted her gently from the chair, and wrapped her into his arms.

Not dramatic.

Not possessive.

Just warm.

Steady.

Safe.

Harper melted into the embrace, pressing her forehead to his shoulder. Snowball jumped onto the stool, tail swishing, pretending she wasn't also emotionally invested.

Jack rubbed her back once, then stepped back just enough to hold her face in his hands.

"You are going to finish this," he said. "I believe that with everything I have."

Harper wiped a tear. "What if you're wrong?"

He smiled softly. "Then we'll be wrong together."

A laugh caught in her throat. "That's not helping."

"Good," he murmured, brushing a stray tear from her cheek. "You needed to laugh."

Harper exhaled. "I'm scared."

"So am I," Jack admitted. "Because I care about you. Because I want you to find the life you deserve. Because I want you here." His voice softened. "But fear isn't a stop sign. It's a compass."

Her eyes met his—wide, vulnerable, clear.

"I don't want to lose this," she whispered.

"You won't," Jack promised.

He kissed her forehead.

Warm.

Steady.

Certain.

"You write," he said gently. "I'll handle everything else."

He moved around the workshop—stoking the fire, straightening her blankets, refreshing her mug. Snowball supervised. Harper sat again, breathing deep.

And slowly—hesitantly—her fingers touched the keys.

A sentence.

Another.

A paragraph.

The scene thawed.

The wall cracked.

And the story flowed again.

[cursor]

Hours later, Jack returned with dinner. Harper barely noticed—she was deep in the chapter, the breakthrough brilliant and fragile.

When she finally looked up, Jack was watching her with a faint, proud smile.

"How's it going?" he asked.

Harper exhaled, a light in her eyes he hadn't seen since she first arrived.

"I think... I'm almost there."

Jack smiled.

And outside, the snow kept falling—steady, quiet, patient—like a world holding its breath just long enough for her to finish.

Chapter 15
The Setback and the Man Who Stays

New Year's Eve dawned pale and cold, the kind of morning where the air bit gently at your cheeks like it was checking if you were awake.

Harper was awake.

She'd written through most of the night, stopping only long enough to shove a granola bar into her mouth and stick her hands under warm water when they cramped. Snowball kept her company on the workshop table, occasionally "editing" by walking directly across the keyboard.

Jack came by at dawn, bringing a thermos of strong coffee and a quiet, proud smile.

"You're close," he murmured, brushing a strand of hair behind her ear.

Harper nodded, vibrating with exhaustion and relief.

"I'm at the last chapter."

Jack's eyes softened, full of awe she wasn't used to seeing directed at her.

"Finish it," he whispered. "I'll keep everything else still."

And he did.

He cleared the snow from her steps.

He brought food she barely remembered eating.

He kept the fire warm.

He kept the world quiet.

Just after noon, Harper paused, fingers trembling over the keys.

Snowball sat up sharply, tail flicking—clearly sensing the shift.

"Jack," Harper called softly. "Jack!"

He was there instantly, brushing sawdust off his hands.

"What's wrong?"

Harper looked up at him, tears welling.

"It's done," she whispered.

"I finished it."

Jack didn't breathe for a moment.

Then he crossed the room in two steps, pulled her into his arms, and spun her once—just once—before setting her gently down.

"You did it," he murmured into her hair. "You beautiful, stubborn, brilliant woman—you did it."

Harper laughed and cried at the same time, clutching at his coat.

"I couldn't have done it without you."

Jack cupped her face. "You did the writing, Harper. You found your voice again."

She swallowed. "But you held the rest of my world steady."

His smile was soft. "Anytime."

They stood like that, breathing each other in, the workshop filled with the quiet glow of triumph.

Then Harper's phone buzzed.

Two words flashed across the screen:

Send manuscript.

Her stomach flipped. "Here we go."

Jack squeezed her hand. "I'm right here."

Harper hit *SEND*.

The file whooshed away into the ether.

A full, polished novel.

Finished in a place she'd come to love with a man she'd come to…

The thought didn't finish.

Because the phone rang.

Harper answered. "Mara?"

Mara didn't speak at first. That was never good.

Finally: "Harper… we might have a problem."

Harper felt the air leave her lungs. "What kind of problem?"

Mara sighed, sounding tired, frustrated, and furious all at once.

"The senior editor—who was supposed to read your manuscript today—just announced she's taking emergency leave. Something about a family crisis. And the stand-in editor wants to push your book… to *late summer*."

Harper blinked hard. "Late… summer? But that means—"

"They'll hold the release," Mara said. "And they'll require a full editorial pass. And they'll want you to come to New York for the revisions."

Jack's jaw tightened as he listened.

Harper closed her eyes, pressing a hand to her forehead.

"This is a nightmare."

"It's not final yet," Mara said quickly. "But I need to fight for you. Hard. And I need you on standby. Can you stay near your phone?"

Harper exhaled shakily. "Yes."

"Good. And Harper? No matter what happens—I'm proud of you."

Harper hung up, numb.

She stared ahead, heart pounding, everything she'd fought for suddenly slipping through her fingers.

"I might have to go back," she whispered.

Jack's breath hitched.

Then he stepped close, taking both her hands in his.

"Harper," he said softly, firmly, as though anchoring her in place, "look at me."

She did.

Those warm, steady eyes held her like a lifeline.

"I told you," he murmured, pressing his forehead to hers, "whatever happens—we'll figure it out. You won't lose me. You won't lose this."

Harper trembled. "But if I have to go—"

"Then I'll wait."

She blinked. "Jack…"

"I have waited for less important things," he said with a soft smile. "And besides—I like the city in spring."

Her breath caught. "You'd come visit?"

"I'd come find you," he said quietly. "Because you matter."

Snowball meowed loudly at that, as if stamping a seal of approval.

Harper laughed shakily, tears streaming now—hope, exhaustion, fear, and love tangled together.

Jack brushed them away with his thumbs.

"No matter what that call says," he murmured, "you're not alone anymore."

Harper leaned into him, letting the warmth of his coat and his arms soothe her trembling heart.

Snow fell quietly outside, thick and gentle, like the world was holding its breath.

The story wasn't finished.

But the ending was coming—

And it was going to be worth it.

Chapter 16
The Choice and the Confession

Harper kept her phone on the table in the workshop, screen up, volume on high, like a bomb waiting to go off.

Every few seconds, she glanced at it.

Then away.

Then back.

Snowball paced like a tiny, irritable bodyguard.

Jack pretended to plane a piece of maple at the far bench, but he kept glancing too—every time Harper's breath hitched, every time her fingers twitched.

Neither of them spoke much.

There was nothing left to say until the call came.

Outside the workshop window, thick snow drifted sideways.

Not a gentle fall now.

A real storm—wind kicking at the eaves, the world dissolving into white.

Harper stared at her manuscript on the table, the printed pages stacked neatly.

Done.

Real.

Hers.

It felt fragile now.

Like something that could slip away at any second.

Her phone buzzed.

Harper froze.

Jack was at her side before she even reached for it.

"Mara," Harper whispered, answering with trembling fingers. "What happened?"

Mara exhaled—long, shaky, a sound Harper had only heard from her once before during a disastrous contract negotiation five years ago.

"Harper," Mara said, voice tight with adrenaline, "we did it."

Harper's knees went out from under her.

Jack caught her by the elbows.

"What—what do you mean?" Harper rasped.

"You're greenlit," Mara said. "Remote."

Harper blinked. "Remote. As in—"

"As in *you get to stay in Cedar Hollow*," Mara said. "No travel. No relocation. All edits and meetings virtual. They accepted your timeline. They think the new book has 'extraordinary emotional clarity.'"

Harper made a choked sound—not quite a laugh, not quite a cry.

"You're serious?"

"As a kidney stone," Mara said. "Harper, sweetheart—congratulations. You pulled a miracle out of a frozen forest. I'm proud of you."

Harper pressed a hand to her chest. "Mara... thank you."

"Go celebrate," Mara said. "Kiss someone on my behalf. I don't care who."

Harper's gaze flicked to Jack's.

Oh.

She knew exactly who.

"Call me tomorrow," Mara added. "We have paperwork."

The call ended.

Harper lowered the phone slowly, like her limbs were made of glass.

Then she looked at Jack.

And everything broke open.

"I get to stay," she whispered.

Jack's breath left him in a visible puff.

"You get to stay," he echoed, voice thick with relief.

Harper laughed—a shaky, disbelieving laugh—and Jack stepped closer, one hand sliding to her waist, the other cupping the back of her head.

"You did it," he murmured.

"No," Harper whispered back, leaning into him. "*We* did."

Snowball chirped, utterly smug.

Jack dipped his forehead to hers, eyes closing. "Harper Lane... I have been trying not to fall for you at the pace of an avalanche, but you're making it extremely difficult."

Harper's fingers curled in his coat.

"Jack."

"I know," he said softly. "You've had too much pressure, too many choices. I didn't want to be another weight on you."

"You're not a weight," Harper whispered. "You're... the opposite."

Jack inhaled, something like hope trembling in the breath. "Tell me."

Harper swallowed hard. Her heart ached with it—the truth, the relief, the dizzying fear.

"You're the reason I could breathe again," she said. "You're the quiet I needed. You're the steadiness I forgot existed. Jack... I didn't just find my writing here."

His eyes opened, soft and luminous.

"What else did you find?" he whispered.

Harper's voice trembled. "You."

Jack's breath hitched.

Then he kissed her.

This one wasn't tentative, or careful, or waiting for the perfect moment.

This one *was* the moment.

Warm and full and breath-stealing.

A kiss like a promise.

A kiss like the world outside the workshop was made entirely of falling snow and soft beginnings.

Harper melted into it, hands sliding into Jack's hair.

Jack pulled her closer, lifting her slightly off her feet as if afraid she might slip away.

Snowball meowed loudly—*finally*—then marched to her blanket and curled up with the air of someone deeply satisfied with her matchmaking.

When they finally parted, both breathless and smiling, Harper whispered:

"So... what now?"

Jack rested his forehead against hers.

"Now?" he murmured.

"Oh, Harper Lane... now everything begins."

And outside, the winter storm raged—a world remaking itself under falling snow.

Chapter 17
The Future in Falling Snow

Harper and Jack stayed in the workshop long after the kiss ended—holding each other, breathing in sync, Snowball snoring gently from her blanket like an exhausted chaperone.

Outside, the storm thickened until the world blurred into white.

Inside, warmth gathered like a second skin.

Harper pulled back just enough to see Jack's face clearly.

"You're really okay with all of this?" she asked softly. "Me staying. The chaos. The deadlines. The… everything?"

Jack's thumb brushed her cheek.

"I didn't fall for a quiet life," he murmured. "I fell for *you*."

Her breath caught. "You make that sound easy."

"It wasn't," he admitted with a crooked smile. "It scared the hell out of me. Still does."

"Why?"

"Because..." His voice dropped, warm and rough. "When you came here, you were like someone holding her breath under ice. And watching you come back to life—Harper, I didn't want to be the reason you sank again. So I waited. And hoped."

Harper's throat tightened. "You didn't save me," she whispered. "You just... stood beside me until I remembered how to swim."

Jack smiled, slow and tender. "Good. Because I plan to keep standing there."

She kissed him again—soft, grateful, threaded with relief.

He wrapped his arms around her, grounding her like the cedar beams around them.

When they finally stepped outside, snowflakes caught in Harper's hair like glitter. Jack held her hand as they walked through the yard toward her house—fresh snow rising around their boots, the storm easing now into gentle laziness.

Cedar Hollow glowed through the storm, lanterns and house lights shining like warm constellations.

"Feels different now," Harper murmured.

Jack squeezed her hand. "Because you're looking forward instead of back."

She laughed softly. "Yeah. I guess I am."

On the porch, he pulled her close again. "You know... Eloise is going to faint when she hears you're staying."

"Oh god," Harper groaned. "She'll schedule a parade."

Jack grinned. "If she does, Snowball will lead it."

As if summoned, Snowball trotted onto the porch railing, tail held high, face full of queenly approval.

Harper scritched under her chin. "Happy now?"

Snowball meowed as if to say *I have always been correct about everything.*

Jack stepped down one step, then turned back to Harper with a look that sent a small, warm earthquake through her chest.

"So," he said. "Tomorrow. Want to start writing the next one?"

Harper blinked. "Next... book?"

Jack shrugged. "Seems like Cedar Hollow is good for your creative process. Might as well start a series."

She laughed and nudged him lightly. "You're impossible."

"I know," he said, leaning in. "But I'm yours to deal with now."

Harper's heart expanded so suddenly she almost swayed.

"Come inside," she whispered. "We'll watch the storm."

Jack brushed a thumb over her lower lip, eyes soft with more than warmth.

"You sure?"

"Yes," Harper said, steady and certain. "I don't want this night to end."

So they went inside.

Snowball marched ahead like royalty.

Jack closed the door behind them.

And the storm raged on outside, while inside the house, two hearts who'd found each other in the winter quiet began warming a future they didn't even know they wanted.

Epilogue, One Year Later

Snow drifted softly outside the Hollow Bookshop. Inside, a small crowd applauded as Harper Lane signed the final copy of her *new* book—

Snowfall at Cedar Hollow.

Eloise dabbed her eyes dramatically.

Mara livestreamed the event from New York, screaming excitedly every few minutes.

Snowball slept on a velvet cushion by the register, wearing a knitted crown.

Jack leaned against a bookcase, watching Harper glow in her element—confident, joyful, home.

When Harper finished the signing, she crossed the room straight into Jack's arms.

"You proud of me?" she asked.

Jack kissed her forehead. "Always."

"Ready to go home?"

He grinned.

"Race you."

They stepped outside into the snow.

Harper took his hand.

Cedar Hollow's lights twinkled around them.

And somewhere above the falling snow, the universe whispered:

Begin again.